Mylo Freeman

Princess *Arabella*

is a Big Sister

CASSAVA | REPUBLIC

Princess Arabella is playing with her ball. She throws it into the air and bounces it up and down. She shakes her curly head. It's a bit boring, she thinks, playing by myself all the time.

Wouldn't it be nicer to have a little brother or a little sister? Someone you could always play with?

"Mom, Dad, I don't want to be an only child any more. Can you get a little brother or sister for me tomorrow? Then we can play together!"

The Queen and King smile and ask, "Which would you prefer?

A little brother or a little sister?"

That's a hard question, thinks Princess Arabella.
A little brother or a little sister?

They both sound like good fun.

A few days later, Princess Arabella is visiting Prince
Mimoun and his sister, Princess Laila.
Mimoun's mom hands out sweets. Mmm, yum yum!

It's really nice having a little sister around,
thinks Arabella.

Suddenly Princess Laila grabs some of her brother's sweets.
"You've got more than me!" she yells.
"I haven't! Give them back!" screams Mimoun.
All of the sweets fall on to the floor.

Hmm, maybe a little brother would be better,
thinks Princess Arabella.

A few weeks later, Arabella goes to play with Princess Ling and her three little brothers.
They decide to do a jigsaw puzzle – with a hundred pieces!
Now there's just one last piece missing.

They can't find the last jigsaw puzzle piece.
"I can see it! I can see it!" cries Princess Ling.
"So now I can put in the last piece!"
"No!" the three brothers all shout together.
"We want to do it!"

They run towards the last piece. And one of them slips and falls… right on top of the puzzle!
Now the puzzle is in a hundred pieces again.
"I wish I didn't have little brothers!" yells Ling.

Maybe I should ask for a big sister instead, Arabella thinks to herself.

A couple of months later, Princess Arabella is playing
dress-up at Princess Sophie's house.

**"Your big sister always wears such pretty
dresses,"** says Arabella with a sigh.
"Why don't we try them on?" says Princess Sophie.

"Shouldn't we ask her first?" replies Arabella.
But Sophie is already diving into Princess Stella's wardrobe.

Princess Arabella and Princess Sophie admire themselves in the mirror.

These dresses are so much prettier than the things in the dressing-up box.

But then Princess Stella storms into the room.

"What are you doing with my clothes?" she shouts.

"Mom! Sophie's playing with my things again!"

It's another couple of months later now.
Princess Arabella still isn't sure.
Would she prefer a little sister or a little brother?

Actually, being an only child is pretty good,
thinks Princess Arabella.

The next morning, Princess Arabella's dad,
the King, wakes her up.
"Wake up, Arabella! Wake up!
It's time! Come and see!"

With sleepy eyes,
Princess Arabella goes into
her mom and dad's
bedroom.

"Look, sweetheart," says the Queen.

"A little brother *and* a little sister! Congratulations, Arabella! You're a big sister now!"